Dear Parent:
Your child's love of reading starts here!

Every child learns to read in a different way and at his or her own speed. Some go back and forth between reading levels and read favorite books again and again. Others read through each level in order. You can help your young reader improve and become more confident by encouraging his or her own interests and abilities. From books your child reads with you to the first books he or she reads alone, there are I Can Read Books for every stage of reading:

SHARED READING
Basic language, word repetition, and whimsical illustrations, ideal for sharing with your emergent reader

BEGINNING READING
Short sentences, familiar words, and simple concepts for children eager to read on their own

READING WITH HELP
Engaging stories, longer sentences, and language play for developing readers

READING ALONE
Complex plots, challenging vocabulary, and high-interest topics for the independent reader

ADVANCED READING
Short paragraphs, chapters, and exciting themes for the perfect bridge to chapter books

I Can Read Books have introduced children to the joy of reading since 1957. Featuring award-winning authors and illustrators and a fabulous cast of beloved characters, I Can Read Books set the standard for beginning readers.

A lifetime of discovery begins with the magical words "I Can Read!"

Visit www.icanread.com for information
on enriching your child's reading experience.

For Peter and Laura
with love!
—A. S. C.

I Can Read Book® is a trademark of HarperCollins Publishers.

Biscuit Loves the Park
Text copyright © 2019 by Alyssa Satin Capucilli
Illustrations copyright © 2019 by Pat Schories
All rights reserved. Manufactured in China.
No part of this book may be used or reproduced in any manner whatsoever without written permission except in the case of
brief quotations embodied in critical articles and reviews. For information address HarperCollins Children's Books, a division of
HarperCollins Publishers, 195 Broadway, New York, NY 10007.
www.icanread.com
Library of Congress Control Number: 2017962474

ISBN 978-0-06-243618-4 (trade bdg.) — ISBN 978-0-06-243617-7 (pbk.)

Typography by Brenda E. Angelilli

18 19 20 21 22 SCP 10 9 8 7 6 5 4 3 2 1   ❖   First Edition

Biscuit
Loves the Park

story by ALYSSA SATIN CAPUCILLI
pictures by PAT SCHORIES

HARPER
An Imprint of HarperCollinsPublishers

Biscuit, where are you?

Woof, woof!

Here, Biscuit.

We're going to play
in the big park.
I have your ball, Biscuit.

Let's play!

Woof, woof!

Wait, Biscuit.

Where are you going?

Your ball is right here.

Let's play!

Woof, woof!

Uh-oh.

There goes the ball!

Woof!

Biscuit, wait for me!

This is a big park.

Woof, woof!

Silly puppy.

Are you by the tree?

Are you by the bench?

Woof, woof!

Biscuit, are you by the pond?

Woof, woof!

Biscuit, where are you?

Woof!

Funny puppy.

Now I found you!

Arf, arf!

Oh, no!

Here, Biscuit!
Here, Biscuit!
I found your ball.
But where can you be?

Woof, woof!
Biscuit, are you by
the merry-go-round?

Are you by the swings?

This is a very big park,
Biscuit.

Where are you?

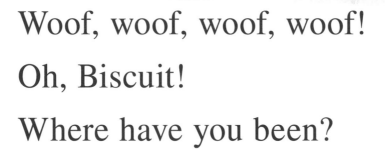

Woof, woof, woof, woof!

Oh, Biscuit!

Where have you been?

I have been looking
for you everywhere.
Woof, woof!

Sweet puppy!

I was trying to find you.

But you found me . . .

and lots of new friends, too.

Now let's play!

Arf!

Ruff!

Woof, woof!